CLEANING UP

Written by Cecilia Minden and Joanne Meier • Illustrated by Bob Ostrom
Created by Herbie J. Thorpe

ABOUT THE AUTHORS

Cecilia Minden, PhD, is the former director of the Language and Literacy Program at the Harvard Graduate School of Education. She is now a reading consultant for school and library publications. She earned her PhD in reading education from the University of Virginia. Cecilia and her husband, Dave Cupp, live outside Chapel Hill, North Carolina. They enjoy sharing their love of reading with their grandchildren, Chelsea and Qadir.

Joanne Meier, PhD, has worked as an elementary school teacher, university professor, and researcher. She earned her BA in early childhood education from the University of South Carolina, and her MEd and PhD in education from the University of Virginia. She currently works as a literacy consultant for schools and private organizations. Joanne lives in Virginia with her husband Eric, daughters Kella and Erin, two cats, and a gerbil.

ABOUT THE ILLUSTRATOR

Bob Ostrom has been illustrating children's books for nearly twenty years. A graduate of the New England School of Art & Design at Suffolk University, Bob has worked for such companies as Disney, Nickelodeon, and Cartoon Network. He lives in North Carolina with his wife Melissa and three children, Will, Charlie, and Mae.

ABOUT THE SERIES CREATOR

Herbie J. Thorpe had long envisioned a beginning-readers' series about a fun, energetic bear with a big imagination. Herbie is a book lover and an avid supporter of libraries and the role they play in fostering the love of reading. He consults with librarians and matches them with the perfect books for their students and patrons. He lives in Louisiana with his wife Misty and their daughter Carson.

Published in the United States of America by The Child's World®
1980 Lookout Drive • Mankato, MN 56003-1705
800-599-READ • www.childsworld.com

Acknowledgments
The Child's World®: Mary Berendes, Publishing Director
The Design Lab: Kathleen Petelinsek, Design;
Gregory Lindholm, Page Production
Assistant colorist: Richard Carbajal

Library of Congress Cataloging-in-Publication Data
Minden, Cecilia.
  Cleaning up / written by Cecilia Minden and Joanne Meier ;
illustrated by Bob Ostrom.
    p. cm. — (Herbster readers)
  Summary: "In this simple story belonging to the second level
of Herbster Readers, young Herbie uses his imagination to get
him through the tedious task of cleaning up his room"—Provided
by publisher.
  ISBN 978-1-60253-011-9 (library bound : alk. paper)
  [1. Imagination—Fiction. 2. Drawing—Fiction. 3. Orderliness—
Fiction. 4. Cleanliness—Fiction. 5. Bears—Fiction.] I. Meier, Joanne
D. II. Ostrom, Bob, ill. III. Title.
  PZ7.M6539Cl 2008
  [E]—dc22   2008002589

Herbie Bear likes to draw.

He likes to draw machines.

He likes to draw trucks.

He likes to draw superheroes.

Herbie likes to color his drawings.

But Herbie does not like to clean up.

Herbie has paper, crayons, trash, and pencils everywhere!

"Good pictures," said Mom,
"but now it is time to clean up."

"Okay," sighed Herbie, "I'll clean up."

"I could draw a machine
to pick up the paper."

"I could draw another machine
to scoop up the crayons."

"I could draw a truck to haul the trash."

"I could draw a superhero to put away the pencils quickly!"

Herbie soon had all his paper, crayons, trash, and pencils put away.

"You did a great job," said Mom.

Herbie just smiled. Cleaning up is easy when you have a little help!